THE EMPEROR'S PAINTING

A Story of Ancient China

by Jessica Gunderson
illustrated by Caroline Hu

PICTURE WINDOW BOOKS
Minneapolis, Minnesota

Editor: Shelly Lyons
Designer: Tracy Davies
Page Production: Melissa Kes
Art Director: Nathan Gassman
Associate Managing Editor: Christianne Jones
The illustrations in this book were created with
brushed pen and ink.

Picture Window Books
151 Good Counsel Drive
P.O. Box 669
Mankato, MN 56002-0669
877-845-8392
www.picturewindowbooks.com

Library of Congress Cataloging-in-Publication Data
Gunderson, Jessica.
The emperor's painting : a story of ancient China / by
Jessica Gunderson ; illustrated by Caroline Hu.
 p. cm. — (Read-it! chapter books: historical tales)
ISBN 978-1-4048-4734-7 (library binding)
1. China—History—Song dynasty, 960-1279—Juvenile
fiction. [1. China—History—Song dynasty, 960-
1279—Fiction. 2. Painting, Chinese—Fiction.] I. Hu,
Caroline, ill. II. Title.
PZ7.G963Em 2008
[Fic]—dc22   2008006305

TABLE OF CONTENTS

WORDS TO KNOW..........................4

INTRODUCTION..........................4

CHAPTER ONE.......................... 5

CHAPTER TWO 15

CHAPTER THREE................... 23

CHAPTER FOUR..................... 31

CHAPTER FIVE 42

CHAPTER SIX 54

AFTERWORD..................... 62

WORDS TO KNOW

arrogant—exaggerating one's own self worth or importance, often in an overbearing manner

calligraphy—artistic or elegant handwriting or lettering

Confucius—a Chinese philosopher whose teachings still influence many Asian citizens and other people around the world

ignorance—the state of lacking knowledge, education, or awareness

Kaifeng—a city located in the Henan province in eastern China

Liu bo—an ancient Chinese game that used pawns and dice; the game backgammon may have evolved from Liu bo

pagoda—a Chinese tower with roofs curving upward at each story; usually built as a temple or memorial

Song Dynasty (A.D. 960-1279)—during this period in China's history, the country's population doubled; the arts flourished during this period

INTRODUCTION

A.D 1120—Song Dynasty

Confucius, the great Chinese thinker, said: "The superior man is confident without being arrogant. The inferior man is arrogant but lacks confidence."

Long ago, when I was a young student, my master, Lin Cho, said to me every morning and every evening, "You, Han Li, are an inferior man."

His words made me angry. I did not think I was inferior! How was I a lesser man? In my mind, I was smarter than even the great Confucius himself!

Lin Cho was known as the smartest master in Kaifeng, but I thought I was smarter. It had taken Lin Cho seven years to learn the characters of the Chinese language, but I learned the characters, all 40,000 of them, in only one year.

I know now that I should have listened to Lin Cho. I should have known that those who do not follow the wisdom of Confucius will never be great men.

4

CHAPTER ONE

Master Lin Cho said, "I am afraid for you, Han Li."

"Afraid? Why? There is nothing that scares me," I boasted. "There is nothing I cannot conquer."

Lin Cho nodded and replied, "Yes. That is why I am afraid."

I ignored him. Instead, I stared at the painting on the wall that Lin Cho was making for Emperor Huizong. The painting was a landscape on a paper scroll. At the top of the scroll, Lin Cho was writing a poem in calligraphy.

The emperor often asked Lin Cho to paint landscapes for him. Lin Cho was known as a great master in Kaifeng, but I knew better. He was no smarter than the birds the fishermen used to catch fish.

The fisherman tied string around a bird's throat so it could not swallow. When the bird caught a fish in its beak, it would have to spit the fish out into the fisherman's  boat. But seconds later, the bird would stick its head into the water again, scoop up a fish, and try to swallow. No matter how many fish the bird caught, its stomach was still empty. The bird never learned—just like Lin Cho.

Lin Cho stepped toward the painting. He was to present it to Emperor Huizong in time for the New Year celebration at the palace. But he wasn't even close to being finished. And the New Year celebration began tomorrow.

"If you let me help you, you'll finish in time," I told Lin Cho.

Lin Cho laughed and said, "You? You will soil the painting with your arrogance. You will offend our great emperor with your fake confidence."

"It is not so!" I cried. "I have perfected poetry, calligraphy, and painting."

It was true. I had reached perfection. Perfection of all three arts was the goal of every scholar.

Lin Cho shook his head. He put down his calligraphy brush. "I must listen for a poem for the emperor," he said, turning to walk out the door. He was going to sit outside in the courtyard until a vision of a poem came to him. When he found the right poem, he could finish the painting.

Lin Cho was no smarter than birds. He did not know that a poem would not come to him in the courtyard. He did not realize that I could help him.

Like everyone in Kaifeng, I had once believed that Lin Cho was a great master.

Every boy wanted to be his student.
And when Lin Cho chose me, I was
grateful. But that was before I began
thinking that I was smarter than
Lin Cho. Soon, I knew more Chinese
characters than he did. My poems
amazed anyone who heard them.

My paintings were the most magnificent
in Kaifeng.

"I should be the one teaching you," I
had once told Lin Cho proudly.

Lin Cho only shook his head. He was
too stubborn to listen to me. He was
always too stubborn to listen to me.

Darkness settled into the room, but Lin Cho did not return from the courtyard.

Finally, I went out to find him. "Lin Cho!" I called.

He was leaning against a wall. When I approached him, he did not rise. I reached out and shook his shoulder. He fell over. And that was when I saw his face.

Lin Cho was ill—very, very ill.

CHAPTER TWO

I helped Lin Cho inside and laid him on the floor. He burned with fever. He didn't wake, even when I splashed cold water on his face.

I knew what had happened. According to Chinese medicine, a person gets ill when yin and yang, two opposing forces, become unbalanced in the body.

I should have called a doctor. But I was afraid Emperor Huizong would find out that Lin Cho was ill. He would be very angry that his painting would not be finished on time.

I needed to keep Lin Cho's illness a secret. I needed to cure him on my own. And I knew I could. I was the smartest boy in Kaifeng.

"Get up, Master," I commanded. But Lin Cho only moaned.

I decided to use my knowledge of medicine to cure him. I soaked tea leaves in hot water. Then I added dried senna leaves. Senna leaves would cleanse his body.

Lin Cho woke long enough to drink the cup of tea. He said nothing. When he was finished, he sank into a very deep sleep.

"Master, wake up!" I urged. "You must finish the painting."

But he slept on, even as the moon rose to shine silver light on his face.

When the morning sun poured into
the room, I again urged Lin Cho to wake.

"Painting," he whispered.

"Yes, you must finish the painting,"
I agreed.

Before the words were out of my
mouth, Lin Cho was fast asleep again.

A loud knock on the door startled me. I covered Lin Cho with another blanket and slowly opened the door. It was Zhou Si-Yong, the imperial doctor.

"Is there illness here?" he asked.

"No, Doctor Zhou," I quickly answered. "My master is working. He is not to be disturbed." Seeing the doubt on the doctor's face, I added proudly, "He is painting for the emperor. I am helping him!"

But Doctor Zhou did not believe me. "Let me in, Han Li," he said.

"No, Doctor Zhou!" I said, shutting the door in his face.

After I heard the doctor's footsteps fade away, I sat down next to Lin Cho. He hadn't moved. And the painting was still unfinished.

I looked at the scattered brushes and the ink drying in the well. I knew what I had to do. I would finish the painting. And it would be the best painting in all of Kaifeng. I was sure of it.

CHAPTER THREE

The morning sun was rising quickly, spreading light over the trees in the courtyard. I didn't have much time. The painting had to be finished by nightfall.

Lin Cho had painted a lake, but I decided the painting needed a mountain. Mountains were my specialty.

There was a loud knock on the door. I knew right away who it was.

"Go away, Doctor Zhou!" I yelled. "I am … I mean, we are working."

"But I have a cure, Han Li!" Dr. Zhou yelled.

I looked at Lin Cho lying still on the floor. He moaned a little.

"No one is ill," I told Doctor Zhou.

Doctor Zhou stopped knocking. I heard his footsteps go slowly down the road.

I settled down to paint my mountain. I could see it perfectly in my mind: a gentle slope at the bottom, the rocky top softened by fog. I began to paint.

In my mind, the mountain had been glorious. On the scroll, the mountain was horrible.

"When the paint dries, it will look better," I told myself. And it did—a little.

Maybe some clouds will help, I thought. I dipped my brush and painted a few clouds across the sky.

In my mind, the clouds had been as soft as pillows. On the scroll, the clouds were lumpy and gray.

I blinked and shook my head. When I looked again, the painting was as magnificent as I had imagined.

I touched my forehead. "I must be getting ill like Lin Cho," I muttered.

The landscape was finished, but I still had to write the poem.

Under the gaze of cloudless skies, Lin Cho had written.

I dipped the pen into the ink and wrote in calligraphy down the side: *Lie the emperor and his marvelous eyes.*

Well, I meant to write *marvelous*. But I could not remember the character for the word. Instead, I had written *lazy*.

The emperor loved poems about himself. He wouldn't notice that I had written *lazy* instead of *marvelous*. He would be so dazzled by the painting's beauty that he wouldn't notice that I had filled Cho's blue skies with clouds.

The sun was now setting. I had to hurry. I rolled the painting under my arm and opened the door. I was face to face with Doctor Zhou.

CHAPTER FOUR

"Doctor Zhou," I said, trying to look very stern.

Behind me, on the floor, Lin Cho moaned loudly.

The doctor's eyes lit up. "I knew it! Lin Cho is ill," he said.

"He is not. He is resting," I said. "He has just finished the emperor's painting."

Doctor Zhou frowned at the painting rolled under my arm.

"Show me," he said.

I shook my head and said, "The emperor is waiting."

Doctor Zhou tugged at the painting, but I pulled it from his grip. He fell to the ground.

I knew that I was to respect my elders. I knew that I should have helped Doctor Zhou to his feet. But instead I ran. I ran past the great Iron Pagoda. I ran past the market where peddlers sold silk, tea, and rice. As I ran, traders, merchants, and scholars stopped to stare.

"What is under your arm?" a little girl asked as I ran past.

"It is a painting for the emperor," I proudly answered.

"Show me," she said.

I slowed to a walk, glancing over my shoulder. Doctor Zhou was not behind me. He was nowhere to be seen.

A small crowd gathered as I unrolled the painted scroll.

"I painted this for the emperor," I said. I held it high for the crowd to see.

The crowd gasped in delight. Well, I *thought* it was delight.

"I am the best artist in Kaifeng!" I said. "I am better than Lin Cho!"

"Han Li!" a voice behind me yelled.

It was Doctor Zhou. I clutched my painting and ran. I didn't stop running until I reached the Huang He River. I hopped into a boat. The river was the quickest way to get from one part of Kaifeng to the other.

"To the palace," I told the boatman. "Quickly, please!"

The river was crowded with boats. All kinds of people—rich and poor, young and old—traveled on the river. The rich people of Kaifeng traveled in boats decorated with jewels. They wore silk clothes of many colors: red, blue, green, and purple. But they didn't wear yellow. Only the emperor wore yellow.

The poor traveled in plain, small boats. They didn't wear silk. They didn't wear any colors except blue and black. But everyone, rich and poor alike, was preparing for the New Year celebration.

I thought of Lin Cho, lying ill on the floor. Would he live to see the New Year? My eyes filled with tears.

I must not cry over old Lin Cho, I thought. But he had been good to me. I remembered all the nights we had spent playing *Liu bo,* my favorite game. I remembered how often he had brought me tea while I studied.

How could I have left Lin Cho to die all alone? I thought.

"Doctor Zhou!" I shouted, hoping he had followed me to the river.

But no one answered. I sank onto the floor of the boat and watched the clouds.

As the boat neared the palace, my
thoughts of Lin Cho washed away.
The setting sun bounced off the silver
pagodas of the palace. Guards stood at
the gates. Servants carried carts of food
through the palace doors.

I imagined what would happen when I presented the painting to the emperor. I imagined his amazement when I told him that *I* had made the painting. Maybe he would bow to me. Maybe he would even make me a palace artist!

CHAPTER FIVE

"I am a student of Lin Cho," I told the guards at the gate. "This is his painting for the emperor."

One guard nodded. "The emperor has been waiting," he said.

I walked through the doors and down

the wide hall. Large stone dragons lined the walls, watching my every move. At the end of the hall was the entrance to the main room, where Emperor Huizong sat among his guests.

I approached the throne and bowed low. When the emperor saw what I carried, he leaped to his feet.

"This is the moment I have been dreaming of," he said. "Show me the painting."

This was the moment I had been dreaming of, too. My hands trembled as I handed the emperor the painting, *my* magnificent painting.

Emperor Huizong unrolled the scroll
and stared. First his face turned as yellow
as his robes. Then his face grew as red as
fire from a dragon's mouth.

"What—" he sputtered.

"I am glad it is to your liking,
Emperor," I said.

"To my liking?" bellowed the emperor.

My heart stopped. "You *do* like it?"
I asked.

"It is worse than the slime at the bottom of the river," he snarled. "It is worse than the slop we feed the pigs."

I bowed to hide my disbelief. My mind spun. If I told Emperor Huizong that I had made the painting, he might throw me in the dungeon—or worse.

"Lin Cho is greatly sorry," I said.

"How could Lin Cho have insulted me like this?" the emperor shouted. "Lin Cho shall never paint again!"

And neither shall I, I thought.

"Wait!" cried a voice from the far end of the room.

I didn't need to turn around to know who it was.

"Lin Cho did not make this painting," Doctor Zhou announced. He pointed at me. "This boy, Han Li, did."

I gulped.

The emperor glared at me. "This boy?" he asked.

"I saw him with my own eyes," explained Doctor Zhou. "His master, Lin Cho, fell ill. Han Li would not let me inside to help. I watched through the window as the boy painted an ugly mountain over Lin Cho's beautiful lake."

"*This* boy?" the emperor repeated,
still glaring.

"Yes," replied Doctor Zhou.

The guests roared. "Punish him!"
they shouted.

"He put clouds in the cloudless sky," a guard told the emperor.

"And he called your eyes lazy," another guard pointed out.

My face burned.

"Throw him into the street," the emperor said finally.

Then he took a knife and sliced my painting in half. "And take this with you!" he shouted as he threw the pieces at me.

I didn't even have time for a farewell bow. The guards scooped me up and carried me past Doctor Zhou, past the guests, and past the dragons. Then they threw me into the street.

I didn't look back as I ran. I didn't even look as brilliant fireworks exploded over the palace, marking the New Year.

Crowds cheered, and a paper dragon danced in the streets.

But I was not cheering. Once, I had been the smartest boy in Kaifeng. Now, I was the saddest.

CHAPTER SIX

I was not sad for long.

When I returned to Lin Cho's, I expected to find him lying ill or even dead. But instead, he was sitting up and smiling.

I rushed to him and squeezed him in a hug. He looked at me, surprised.

I backed away and gave him a low bow, like any boy should when greeting his elders.

Lin Cho laughed. "I am not surprised that you have forgotten your manners," he said. "I am surprised that you have hugged me."

"I was worried," I admitted.

"While you were gone, Doctor Zhou came by and cured me," Lin Cho said.

"He was a busy man today," I muttered.

Lin Cho raised his eyebrows. He looked at the empty wall where the painting had hung. "You delivered my painting to the emperor?" he asked.

I slowly lowered my head in shame.

I explained what had happened. But instead of punishing me, Lin Cho only nodded gravely.

"I will paint the emperor another one," he said.

And he did. Lin Cho made many, many more paintings, each one more beautiful than the last. All of them hung in the emperor's sparkling palace. Lin Cho remained the best scholar and artist in Kaifeng.

Yes, he was better than I was. I will admit it now.

It took many years of study before I
was able to paint or write poetry again.
The miserable painting I had done for
the emperor had revealed my ignorance.
I had to start again from the beginning.

I had to learn how to be confident instead of arrogant.

I am an older master now, and I often see the arrogance of my students.

They remind me of myself as a child.

"The superior man is confident without being arrogant," I tell them, just as Confucius once said, and just as Lin Cho used to tell me.

And I know they will learn someday.

AFTERWORD

China is home to some of the oldest literature and art in the world. From ancient times, visual art and poetry have held great importance in Chinese culture. The arts flourished during the Song Dynasty (A.D. 960–1279). Emperor Huizong of the Song Dynasty was a talented poet and painter. He even invented his own style of calligraphy known as "slender gold."

Landscapes were the most popular form of painting in Ancient China. Emperors and others who lived in cities wished to bring the peace of the countryside into their homes. Often poetry was written in calligraphy upon the landscape. Calligraphy itself was considered a form of visual art.

Artists and scholars studied many years to learn Chinese characters. The Chinese language has more than 40,000 characters. Each character represents one word. The characters are written using calligraphy. Artists who perfected the calligraphy often knew each character by heart.

Paintings were done on silk or paper scrolls. The silk or paper was prepared with a fine coating of clay or plaster. This made the surface smooth and firm.

Ancient Chinese painting was often done using just ink and paper. Paintings on silk were very expensive and often done for royal funerals.

Emperor Huizong was a great supporter of the arts. He left a lasting influence on the importance of art in Chinese culture.

Huang He River

Kaifeng

SONG DYNASTY
in A.D. 1120

ON THE WEB

FactHound offers a safe, fun way to find Web sites related to topics in this book. All of the sites on FactHound have been researched by our staff.

1. Visit *www.facthound.com*
2. Type in this special code: 1404847340
3. Click on the FETCH IT button.

Your trusty FactHound will fetch the best sites for you!

LOOK FOR MORE *READ-IT!* READER CHAPTER BOOKS: HISTORICAL TALES:

The Actor, the Rebel, and the Wrinkled Queen
The Blue Stone Plot
The Boy Who Cried Horse
The Gold in the Grave
The Jade Dragon
The Lion's Slave
The Magic and the Mummy
The Maid, the Witch, and the Cruel Queen
The Phantom and the Fisherman
The Plot on the Pyramid
The Prince, the Cook, and the Cunning King
The Secret Warning
The Shepherd and the Racehorse
Stranger on the Silk Road
The Terracotta Girl
The Thief, the Fool, and the Big Fat King
The Torchbearer
The Tortoise and the Dare
The Town Mouse and the Spartan House